Home for a Penguin, Home for a Whale

written by **Brenda Williams**

illustrated by **Annalisa Beghelli**

Barefoot Books
Step inside a story

Creeping crab, when all alone,
Hides itself beneath a stone.

Glowing jellyfish, round and wide,
Drifts ashore on breaking tide.

Flightless penguin, waddling free,
Dips and dives in icy sea.

Wide-winged albatross sleeps afloat,
But breeds on islands quite remote.

Huge blue whale with swiftest motion,
Travels far in every ocean.

Great white shark gives toothy grin,
To lure the little fishes in.

Wandering polar bear,
white as snow,
slumbers on a cold ice floe.

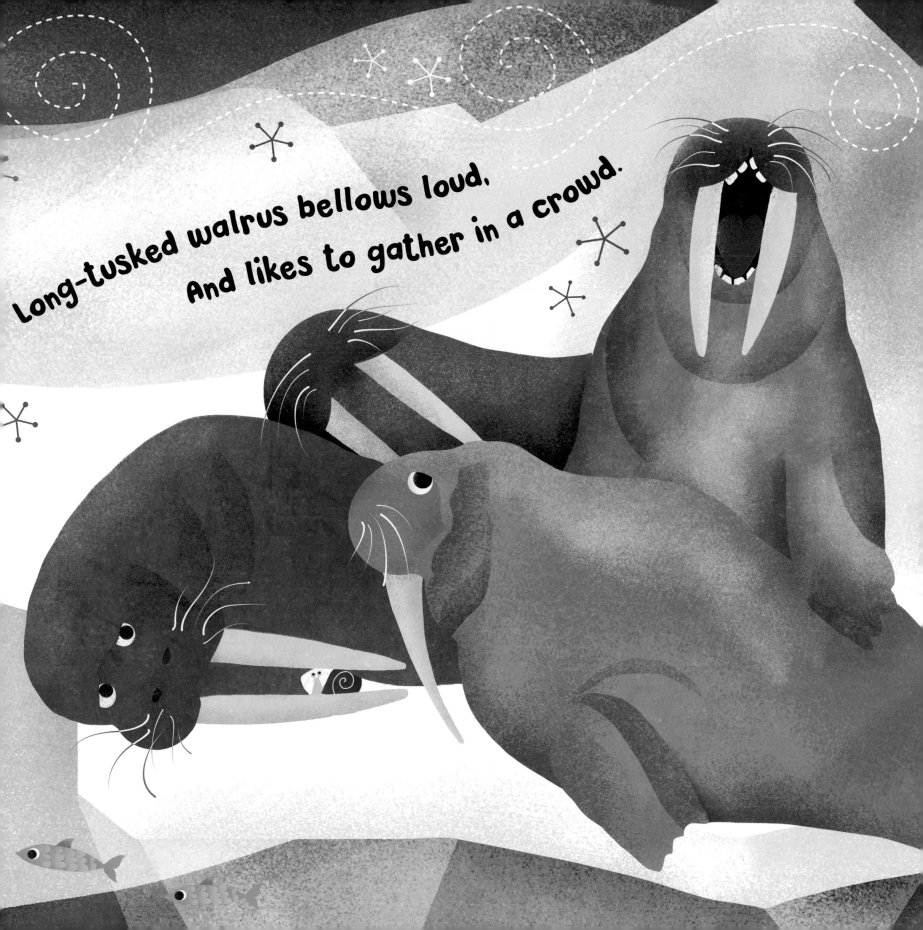

Long-tusked walrus bellows loud,
And likes to gather in a crowd.

Dainty seahorse, small and frail,
Holds onto coral with its tail.

Cunning octopus in disguise,
Blends with backgrounds, to surprise.

Sneaky barracuda strikes at speed,
Through coral reefs and mangrove trees.

Pelican's pouch is deep and wide,
with room for lots of fish inside.

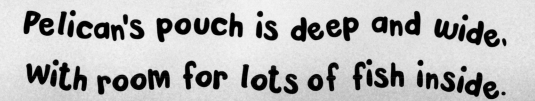

Dolphin leaps and dives in play,
But uses sound to catch its prey.

Manta ray appears to fly,
But no one knows the reason why.

Orca's teeth are sharp and long.
It talks by singing secret songs.

Seal can dive in seas quite deep,
But lies on rocks to rest and sleep.

Flying fish can leap and glide,
Above the sea, with fins stretched wide.

Sea snail has a pretty shell,
Which is its home and guards it well.

sea otter dines while on its back,
using its stomach to hold a snack.

sea urchin can be large or tiny,
But it is always round and spiny.

Lobster hides in rocks and weeds,
But hunts at night for the food it needs.

And here beside the surf and foam,
I just love my seaside home!

More Sea Creature Facts!

Crabs have ten legs. They use one pair as claws or pincers to communicate, catch their prey and protect themselves. They live in most oceans and rock pools on beaches, where they can hide under rocks for safety. They can also scuttle sideways to escape from animals that are trying to eat them.

Sea star is the more accurate name for starfish, as they are not actually fish. Most sea stars have five arms. If they lose an arm, they have the amazing ability to regrow it. When they die, their bodies harden into a shell-like material. They live in shallow, warm waters.

Jellyfish exist in many beautiful shades of the rainbow and have lived in our oceans since before dinosaurs roamed the earth. They use their stinging tentacles to stun other sea creatures before eating them, and they can also give a nasty sting to swimmers. They live in most oceans.

Penguins live in the Southern Hemisphere. The most common penguins in the Antarctic Ocean are the Adélie and the Emperor. Adélies are much smaller than Emperors and make nests by building stones into a small mound. Male Emperor penguins carry their eggs on their feet to protect them and keep the eggs warm.

Albatross have enormous wings of up to 3m (10ft) across and can fly thousands of miles in one journey. Scientists think they may actually sleep while gliding on the air, to save energy. They have also been seen sleeping on the surface of the water. They live mainly in the Antarctic and North Pacific Oceans.

Did you find the hidden sea snail in every scene in this book?

Blue whales are the largest creatures that have ever lived on this planet — even larger than the dinosaurs. Blue whales visit oceans near the North and South Poles in summer but move to warmer oceans to breed in winter. They can spout water into the air higher than any other whale.

Great white sharks live in most warmer waters. When they are young, they feed on small fish. But when they're older, they prefer to eat sea mammals, especially seals. Sharks rarely harm people. In fact, they are actually endangered by humans who hunt them.

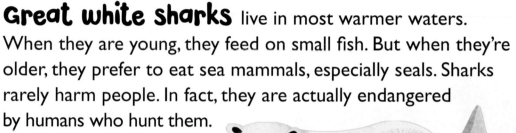

Polar bears live around the North Pole. They are the largest of all bears, and they are fierce hunters that like to be alone. When hungry, they will eat almost any available animal, including reindeer. They can spend hours patiently sitting beside small holes in the ice, waiting to catch a seal as it comes to the surface to breathe.

Walruses are very social creatures that enjoy lying on the ice with hundreds of others, calling loudly to one another. But males can be aggressive, using their enormous tusks to fight. They live in and around the Arctic Ocean.

Seahorses live in warmer waters and coral reefs. They can wrap their tail around coral or weeds, so they are not carried away by strong sea currents. Seahorses can link their tails together in pairs. They can also camouflage, which means changing appearance to blend in with their surroundings.

Octopuses can live in most oceans, but they prefer coral reefs. Like seahorses, they use camouflage to make themselves hard to find. Octopuses build their nests in cracks between underwater rocks, but they do not like to stay in one place for long. They usually build a new home after about two weeks.

Barracudas are ferocious fish that live in warm waters near the shore. They can grow to about 2m (6.5ft) in length and have sharp, pointed teeth. When hunting, they can lie perfectly still for hours, then move quickly to attack their prey.

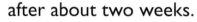

Pelicans have the largest bills of all birds. Their pouch can hold more than 10L (3 gal) of water — as well as fish to eat! Pelicans build their nests on land, near the shore. Their webbed feet help them to move in water.

Dolphins live in large groups called pods. They use body language and make whistles and clicks to communicate with each other. To catch their prey, they use echolocation, which means listening for sounds that bounce off nearby objects. Dolphins live in all oceans but like warmer waters best.

Manta rays can breach, or launch themselves out of the water. With their flat bodies and fin-like wings, they can actually fly through the air for a short time. They might re-enter the sea head first or tail first. Sometimes they even do a somersault! Manta rays live in warm waters.

Orcas (also known as killer whales) are a type of dolphin found in all oceans. They hunt together in large pods, working together to catch their prey. They eat seals, sea lions and even whales.

Seals live in the oceans of the Northern Hemisphere. They feed at sea but haul themselves out onto rocky islands or shorelines to rest or give birth. Although they move awkwardly on land, they swim gracefully and speedily in water. One species of seal has ears that close when they dive underwater.

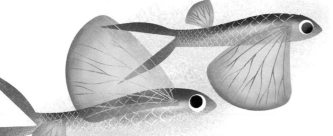

Flying fish have long wing-like fins that they use to leap out of the sea and glide through the air. This helps them escape from animals that are hunting them. They live in warm waters near the Equator.

Sea otters sleep in the sea and, like seals, move more awkwardly on land. They often float on their backs, using their stomachs as a table for their food. They use rocks to crack the shells of clams and other creatures they eat. They live near the shore in the North Pacific Ocean.

Sea snails are molluscs, which means they have no backbone but have a soft body covered by a protective shell. They can live in all the oceans but prefer coral reefs. When they die, their shell drops to the bottom of the sea and might later wash up on the shore.

Sea urchins live on the rocky bottom of warm oceans, especially in shallow waters. They also live in coral reefs. Sea urchins use suckers on their feet to move around on the sea floor. Their spines protect them and help them collect food.

Lobsters live in all the oceans. They hide in cracks or burrows on the sea floor during the day but come out at night to hunt for small fish, snails, mussels and worms. They shed their shells many times as they grow larger.

Oceans

The **Atlantic Ocean** is the world's second-largest ocean. The equator separates the North Atlantic Ocean and the South Atlantic Ocean. The Atlantic contains an enormous underwater mountain range called the Mid-Atlantic Ridge.

The **Pacific Ocean** is the largest and deepest ocean in the world. Like the Atlantic Ocean, it is split by the Equator into the North Pacific Ocean and the South Pacific Ocean. The water is colder near the North and South Poles and warmer near the Equator.

The **Antarctic or Southern Ocean** surrounds Antarctica, the most southern continent. It is very cold and windy. Antarctica is the biggest piece of ice on Earth's surface.

North America

ATLANTIC

South America

PACIFIC

SOUTHERN

Habitats

Estuaries form at the wide mouth of a river, where it meets and mixes with the sea. The water in estuaries is salty, but not as salty as seawater. Mangrove forests sometimes grow here and help protect coastlines.

Coral reefs are formed by the skeletons of tiny animals called polyps. Reefs are extremely important because they protect coastlines from strong waves and storms. They come in all shades of the rainbow, thanks to tiny water plants called algae!

ARCTIC

Europe

Asia

PACIFIC

Africa

INDIAN

Oceania

Antarctica

The **Arctic Ocean** is the smallest and shallowest of the five major oceans. The area around the North Pole is called the Arctic. Some parts of the Arctic are covered by ice or snow all year round.

The **Equator** is a line we draw on maps to divide the earth into two equal parts, called the North and South Hemispheres.

The **Indian Ocean** is the warmest and third-largest ocean of them all. The water is at such a high temperature that many animals struggle to survive in it.

Lagoons are shallow pools of water near the coast, separated from the sea by coral reefs or sand bars. Since the water is so shallow, they can flood or dry out completely when sea levels change.

Sea ice forms when parts of the ocean freeze, especially near the North and South Poles, where it's very cold and cloudy year-round. Animals such as polar bears, seals and penguins live on sea ice.

Climate Change & Clean Energy

Climate change or "global warming" means that the planet's temperatures are rising. As the planet gets warmer, the oceans also become warmer, which can be unsafe for many of the creatures that live there. For example, climate change can destroy coral reefs. When warm temperatures kill the bright algae that live inside the coral, the coral turns white. This is called bleaching.

Higher temperatures are also melting the large sheets of ice, called ice caps, at the North and South Poles. This leaves animals like seals and polar bears without homes. When ice caps melt, they also add more water to the oceans, causing the oceans to overflow and flood beaches and estuaries.

Most scientists agree that climate change is caused by humans using fuels like oil and coal, which release gases into the air. These gases act as a huge blanket over the planet, trapping in heat.

But here's the good news: Now that we know what causes climate change, we can help prevent it from getting worse. Scientists are exploring ways to create energy using the wind, sun and water instead of oil and coal. This is called "clean energy" because it causes much less pollution.

Plastic Dumping & Recycling

Humans create more than 300 million tons of plastic each year, and dump eight million tons of it into the world's oceans. Sea creatures often get caught in plastic netting or think plastic is food and eat it, which can kill them. Plastic also lasts for a very long time. So, if people keep dumping the same amount of plastic in the ocean each year, there could be more plastic than fish there by the year 2050!

In many countries, it is already illegal to dump plastic into the ocean. Some countries are even working on ways to replace straws, shopping bags and other single-use plastic items that often end up polluting the water.

Keep our oceans clean!

- If you see plastic waste outdoors, ask an adult to help you recycle it
- Carry a reusable water bottle with you instead of buying disposable plastic water bottles
- Avoid using plastic straws if possible
- Bring your own reusable bags when you go shopping
- Ask your family to buy food without plastic packaging whenever possible

With love to Evie, Lily and Sophie — B.W.

Thanks to Valentino and my little ones
Olivia and Nora, my family and my
friends who believe in me — A.B.

Barefoot Books
2067 Massachusetts Ave
Cambridge, MA 02140

Barefoot Books
29/30 Fitzroy Square
London, W1T 6LQ

Text copyright © 2019 by Brenda Williams
Illustrations copyright © 2019 by Annalisa Beghelli
The moral rights of Brenda Williams and Annalisa Beghelli have been asserted

First published in the United States of America by Barefoot Books, Inc
and in Great Britain by Barefoot Books, Ltd in 2019
All rights reserved

Graphic design by Sarah Soldano, Barefoot Books
Edited and art directed by Lisa Rosinsky, Barefoot Books
Reproduction by Bright Arts, Hong Kong
Printed in China on 100% acid-free paper
This book was typset in Pardesi and Popsicle
The illustrations were prepared digitally using a graphic pen and tablet

Hardback ISBN 978-1-78285-743-3
Paperback ISBN 978-1-78285-744-0
E-book ISBN 978-1-78285-759-4

British Cataloguing-in-Publication Data:
a catalogue record for this book is available from the British Library
Library of Congress Cataloging-in-Publication Data
is available under LCCN 2018043303

1 3 5 7 9 8 6 4 2

Barefoot Books
step inside a story

At Barefoot Books, we celebrate art and story that opens the hearts
and minds of children from all walks of life, focusing on themes that
encourage independence of spirit, enthusiasm for learning and respect
for the world's diversity. The welfare of our children is dependent on
the welfare of the planet, so we source paper from sustainably managed
forests and constantly strive to reduce our environmental impact.
Playful, beautiful and created to last a lifetime, our products combine
the best of the present with the best of the past to educate our
children as the caretakers of tomorrow.

www.barefootbooks.com